10/15/09

8.95

The Prince and the Pauper

SAMUEL CLEMENS

D1534294

WITHDRAWN

SADDLEBACK
PUBLISHING · INC.

Saddleback's *Illustrated Classics*™

Three Watson
Irvine, CA 92618-2767
Website: www.sdlback.com

Copyright © 2006 by Saddleback Publishing, Inc. All rights reserved. No part of this book may be reproduced in any form or by any means, electronic or mechanical, including photocopying, recording, or by any information storage and retrieval system, without the written permission of the publisher.

ISBN 1-56254-930-8

Printed in China

Welcome to
Saddleback's *Illustrated Classics*™

We are proud to welcome you to Saddleback's *Illustrated Classics*™. Saddleback's *Illustrated Classics*™ was designed specifically for the classroom to introduce readers to many of the great classics in literature. Each text, written and adapted by teachers and researchers, has been edited using the Dale-Chall vocabulary system. In addition, much time and effort has been spent to ensure that these high-interest stories retain all of the excitement, intrigue, and adventure of the original books.

With these graphically *Illustrated Classics*™, you learn what happens in the story in a number of different ways. One way is by reading the words a character says. Another way is by looking at the drawings of the character. The artist can tell you what kind of person a character is and what he or she is thinking or feeling.

This series will help you to develop confidence and a sense of accomplishment as you finish each novel. The stories in Saddleback's *Illustrated Classics*™ are fun to read. And remember, fun motivates!

Overview

Everyone deserves to read the best literature our language has to offer. Saddleback's *Illustrated Classics*™ was designed to acquaint readers with the most famous stories from the world's greatest authors, while teaching essential skills. You will learn how to:

• Establish a purpose for reading
• Use prior knowledge
• Evaluate your reading
• Listen to the language as it is written
• Extend literary and language appreciation through discussion and writing activities

Reading is one of the most important skills you will ever learn. It provides the key to all kinds of information. By reading the *Illustrated Classics*™, you will develop confidence and the self-satisfaction that comes from accomplishment—a solid foundation for any reader.

Step-By-Step

The following is a simple guide to using and enjoying each of your *Illustrated Classics*™. To maximize your use of the learning activities provided, we suggest that you follow these steps:

1. *Listen!* We suggest that you listen to the read-along. (At this time, please ignore the beeps.) You will enjoy this wonderfully dramatized presentation.

2. *Pre-reading Activities.* After listening to the audio presentation, the pre-reading activities in the Activity Book prepare you for reading the story by setting the scene, introducing more difficult vocabulary words, and providing some short exercises.

3. *Reading Activities.* Now turn to the "While you are reading" portion of the Activity Book, which directs you to make a list of story-related facts. Read-along while listening to the audio presentation. (This time pay attention to the beeps, as they indicate when each page should be turned.)

4. *Post-reading Activities.* You have successfully read the story and listened to the audio presentation. Now answer the multiple-choice questions and other activities in the Activity Book.

Remember,

"Today's readers are tomorrow's leaders."

Samuel Clemens

Samuel Langhorne Clemens, an American novelist, wrote under the pen name of Mark Twain. He is known as one of the major authors of American fiction and the greatest humorist in American literature. He was born in 1835 in Florida, Missouri. His family moved to Hannibal, Missouri, a village on the Mississippi River in 1839. His father died in debt in 1847, and Samuel Clemens went to work for a newspaper and printing firm.

He had little formal education, learning what he needed to know while working in the printing business. In 1857, Clemens decided to become a riverboat pilot. His pen name, *Mark Twain,* comes from a riverboat term meaning *two fathoms* (a depth of 12 feet, or 3.7 meters).

In 1861, the Civil War stopped commercial boat traffic on the Mississippi, and Clemens left the river.

He wrote many books among them, *The Adventures of Tom Sawyer* and the *Adventures of Huckleberry Finn,* which was a sequel to *Tom Sawyer.* The book *The Prince and the Pauper* is a story of what happens when a young Prince Edward and a poor boy trade identities.

Samuel Clemens died in 1910.

Saddleback's *Illustrated Classics*™

The Prince and the Pauper

SAMUEL CLEMENS

THE MAIN CHARACTERS

King Henry VIII

Miles Hendon

The Prince

The Pauper

John Canty

Mrs. Canty

In the old city of London, during the sixteenth century, a son was born to the poor Canty family. They already had more children than they could feed and they weren't happy about having one more.

On the same day another child was born —this time to the royal family. Indeed, all of England was filled with joyous talk of the new baby, Edward Tudor, the Prince of Wales.

This story has been told and retold, passed from parent to child for three hundred years or more. The two boys, a prince and a pauper, looked so much alike that when a trick of fate changed them around, not even their own families could tell who was who.

8

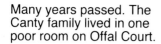

Many years passed. The Canty family lived in one poor room on Offal Court.

There, drinking and fighting were a way of life.

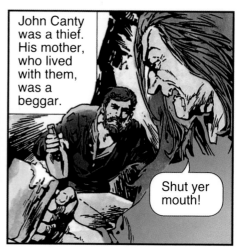

John Canty was a thief. His mother, who lived with them, was a beggar.

Shut yer mouth!

They made beggars of the children but could not force them to steal. When young Tom came home with no money, his father would beat him.

I'll teach you to come home without a penny, you brat.

But in the night his mother would come to him with some soup or a crust of bread she had saved by going hungry herself.

Here, my darling, eat this.

Yet little Tom was a happy child. He thought that everyone lived the way his family did.

There was fun enough for all.

The boys had foot races, swam in the rivers, and even had grand mud fights.

A kind old priest named Father Andrew lived nearby. He taught Tom how to read and write, and even gave him a few lessons in Latin.

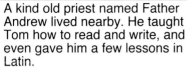

Amo, amas, amat...

Very good, lad.

He filled Tom with tales of giants, princes, and kings, till Tom's head grew full of those wonderful old stories.

Many a night Tom lay in the dark, tired and hungry.

But he dreamed of princes and castles.

In his hours of play, Tom pretended that he lived in the king's court. He was the prince; his friends were the lords and ladies.

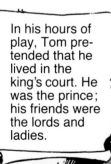

The royal army awaits your orders, your highness.

One morning as Tom walked through the city, he found himself in front of the king's palace at Westminster.

Poor little Tom in his rags caught sight of a handsome boy inside the gate. His clothes were of silk and satin and they shone with jewels. Tom pressed his face against the bars.

It is the prince himself!

Then, suddenly...

Mind your manners, you young beggar!

The crowd laughed, but young prince Edward jumped forward.

How dare you treat a poor boy like that. Open the gates and let him in!

You look tired and hungry. Come with me.

Edward took Tom inside the palace. At his order, the most wonderful breakfast that Tom had ever seen was set before him.

Thank you, my prince.

The prince asked Tom all about himself.

Is your life happy?

In truth, yes, except when I am hungry.

Tell me more about the way you live.

Out in the streets there are Punch and Judy shows, and plays, and foot races.

In the summer we swim in the rivers.

How wonderful! If I could swim in a river just once...

12

And if I could be dressed in your beautiful clothes—just once...

Then so it shall be!

A few minutes later they stood before a great mirror. Tom was dressed in the grand clothes of the prince and the prince was dressed in Tom's rags.

We look exactly alike: same hair, same eyes, same voice. No one could tell, except by our clothes, who is Prince Edward of Wales and who is poor Tom.

But what is this mark on your hand?

Oh, that was given to me by the guard at the gate.

How dare he do that? Wait here until I return!

But when Edward reached the gate, the guard gave him a hard blow that knocked him to the ground.

Take that, young beggar, for the trouble you've caused me!

But I am the Prince of Wales!

Be off, you brat!

And so, a strange thing came to pass...

Make way for his royal highness! Ha, ha, ha!

As the day wore on, the homeless prince made his way through the streets of the city.

I must find Offal Court. Tom's family will surely help me.

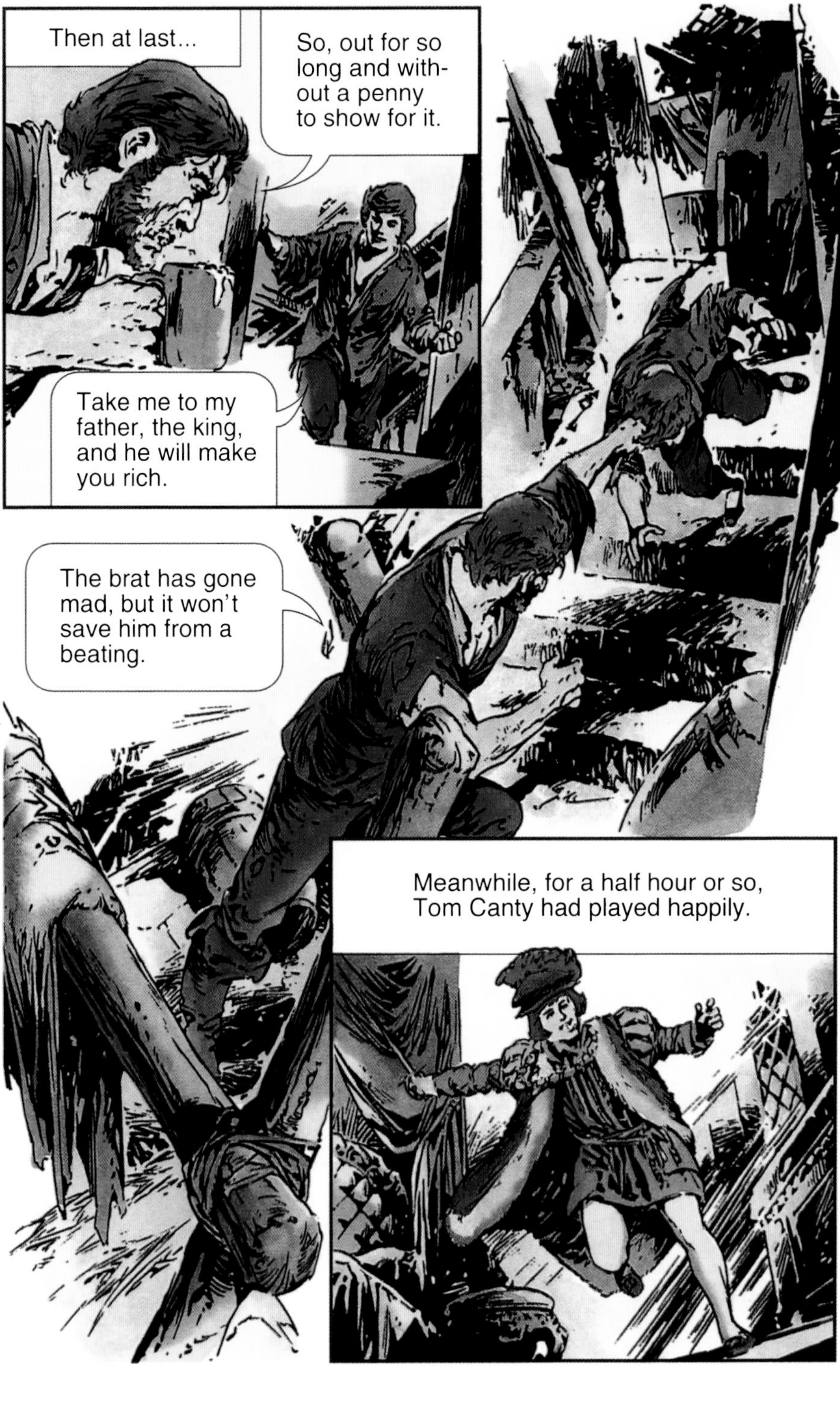
Then at last...
So, out for so long and without a penny to show for it.
Take me to my father, the king, and he will make you rich.
The brat has gone mad, but it won't save him from a beating.
Meanwhile, for a half hour or so, Tom Canty had played happily.

But at last he grew tired—and frightened as well—when the prince did not return.

What will become of me?

Only moments later...

The lady Jane Grey.

Please help me. Give me back my own clothes, for I am not a prince.

Heaven help us! The prince has gone mad!

It was not long before the king heard this news. He called to see his son.

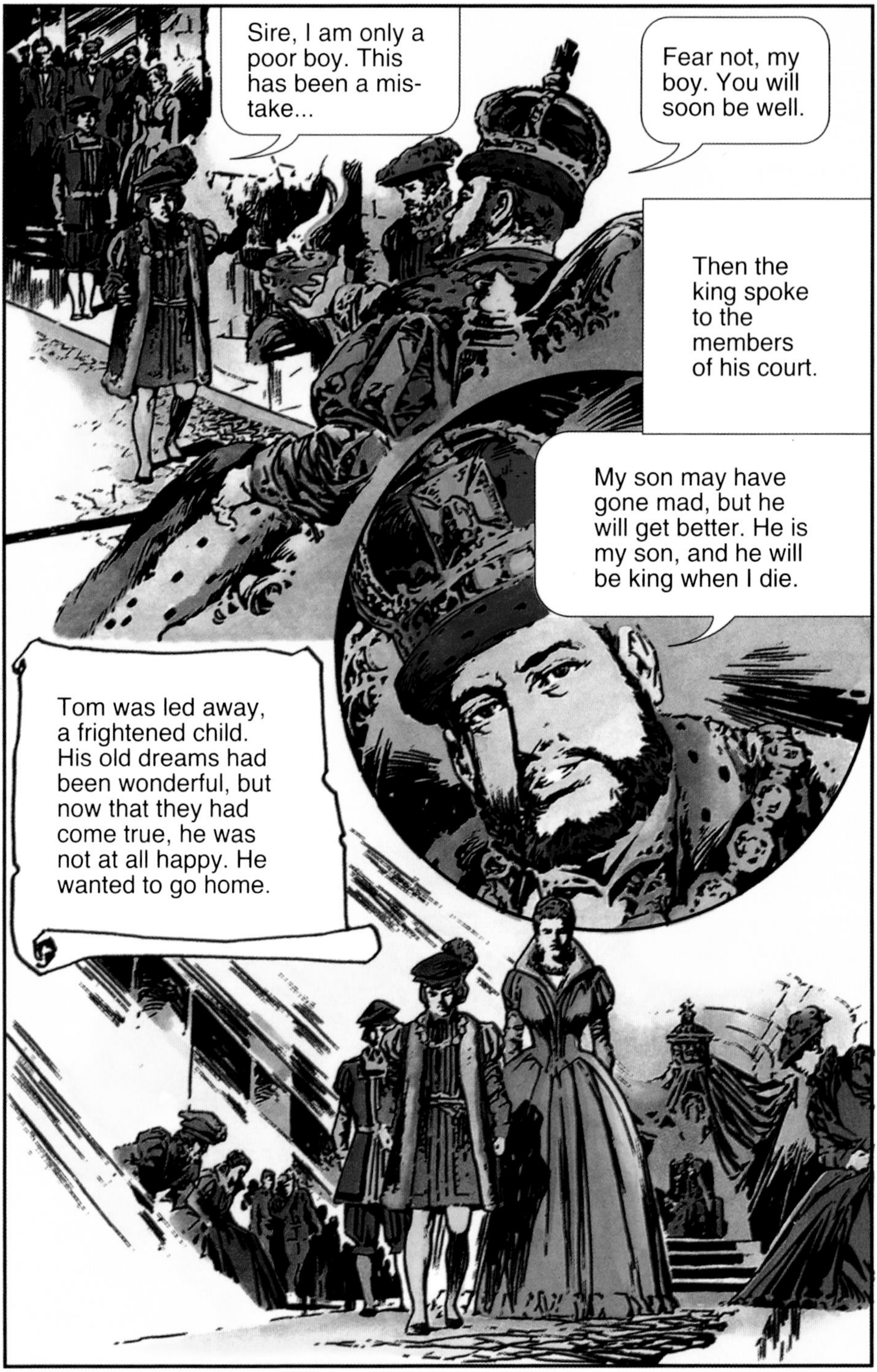
Sire, I am only a poor boy. This has been a mis-take...
Fear not, my boy. You will soon be well.
Then the king spoke to the members of his court.
My son may have gone mad, but he will get better. He is my son, and he will be king when I die.
Tom was led away, a frightened child. His old dreams had been wonderful, but now that they had come true, he was not at all happy. He wanted to go home.

Shortly after noon Tom was given his second meal of the day. If any in the room were upset that he ate with his fingers, they did not show it.

Back in his own rooms, Tom came across a book that he knew would help him. Quickly he began to read.

It was well that he had done so, for that evening he attended the mayor's banquet. With him came the princess Elizabeth and the lady Jane Grey.

Meanwhile, on the other side of the city, the real prince was being dragged into Offal Court. Only one person tried to help him.

Have mercy!

It was old Father Andrew. In his anger, John Canty did not recognize the priest and turned toward him, raising his club.

This is none of your business, old man. Take that!

When they reached home...

Now tell me again. Who are you?

I am Edward, Prince of Wales, and none other.

Poor Tom. All that reading has made you mad. Am I not your mother?

I do not mean to hurt you, but truly I have never looked upon your face before.

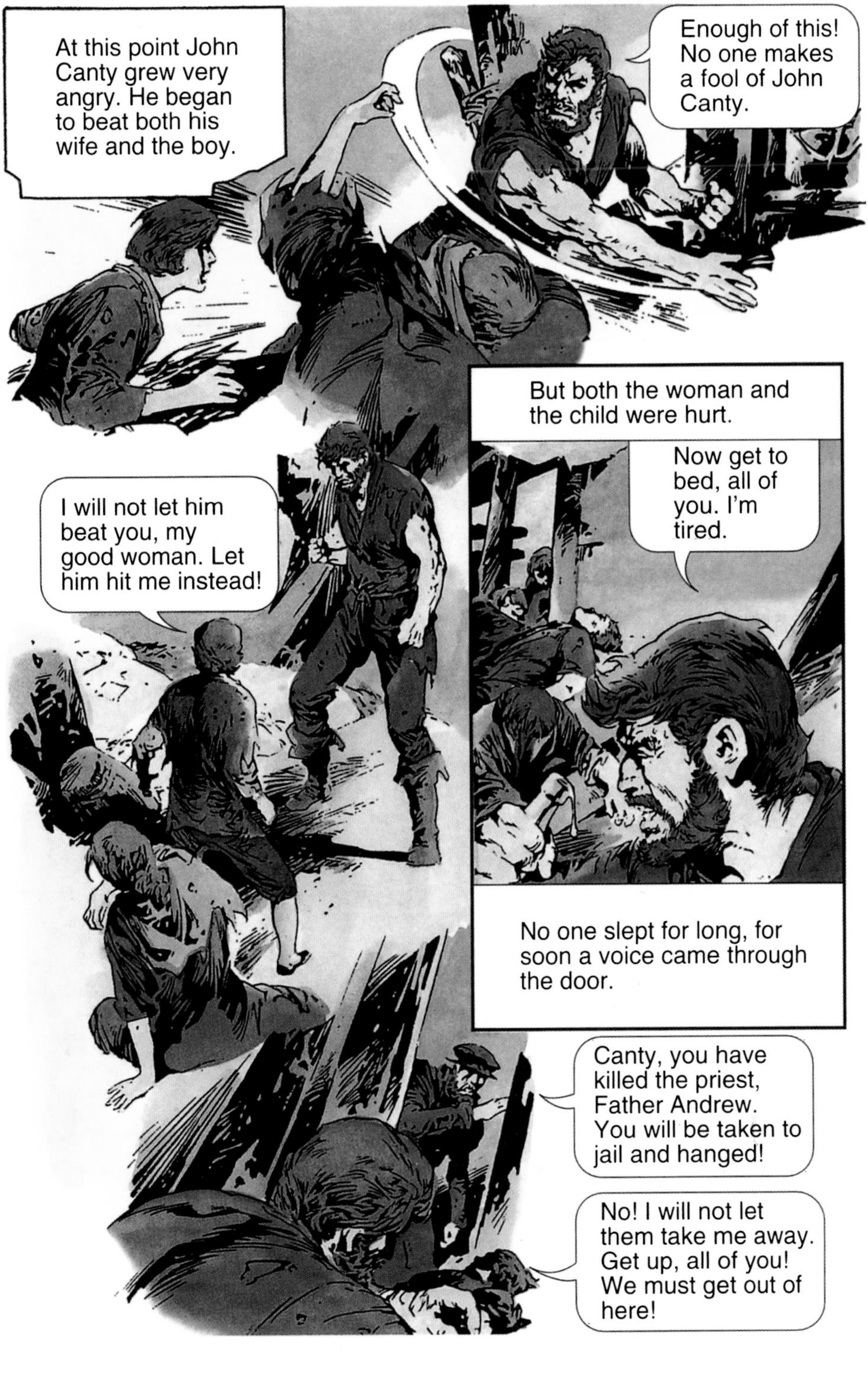

At this point John Canty grew very angry. He began to beat both his wife and the boy.
Enough of this! No one makes a fool of John Canty.
I will not let him beat you, my good woman. Let him hit me instead!
But both the woman and the child were hurt.
Now get to bed, all of you. I'm tired.
No one slept for long, for soon a voice came through the door.
Canty, you have killed the priest, Father Andrew. You will be taken to jail and hanged!
No! I will not let them take me away. Get up, all of you! We must get out of here!

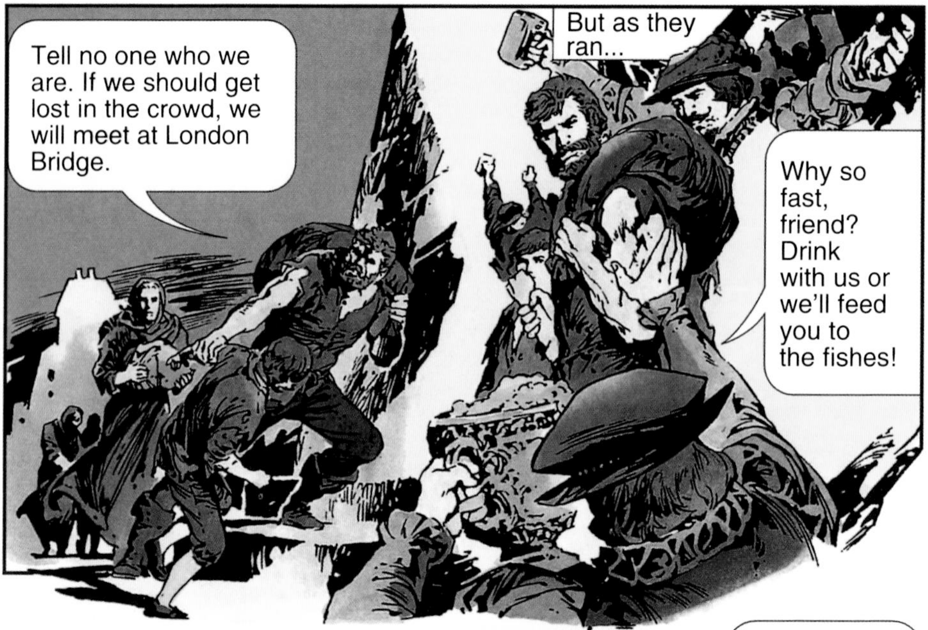
Tell no one who we are. If we should get lost in the crowd, we will meet at London Bridge.
But as they ran...
Why so fast, friend? Drink with us or we'll feed you to the fishes!

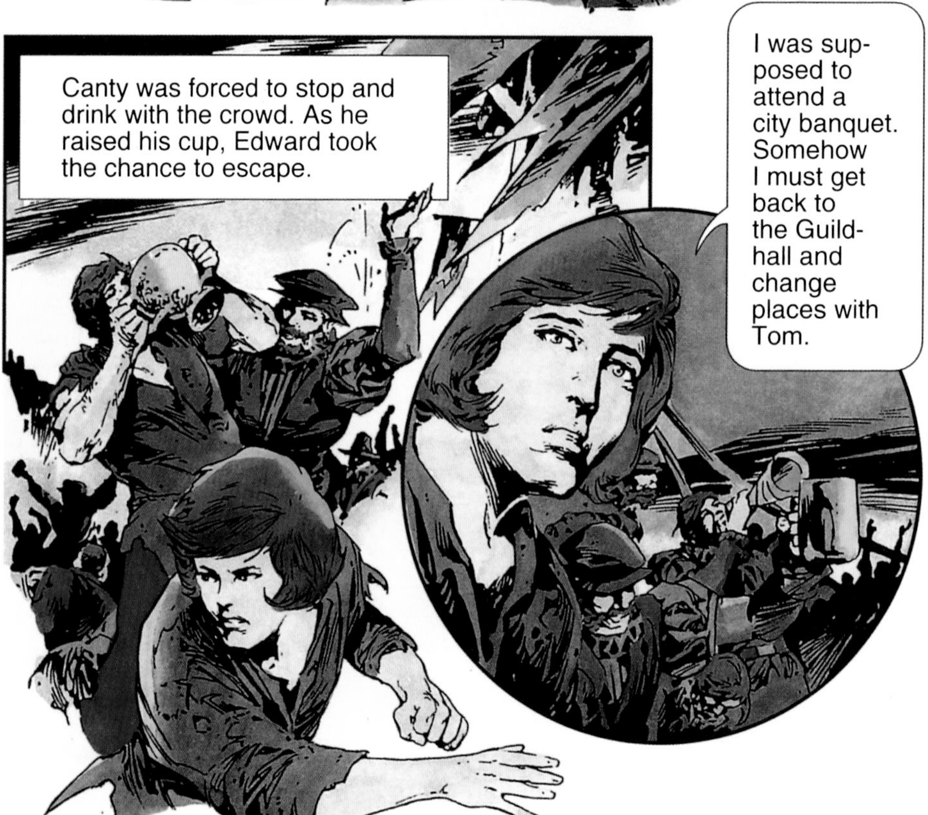
Canty was forced to stop and drink with the crowd. As he raised his cup, Edward took the chance to escape.
I was supposed to attend a city banquet. Somehow I must get back to the Guildhall and change places with Tom.

But when he reached the hall, no one would let him in.

Make way! I am your prince!

Ha! Let's throw the fool in the river!

Just then, help came in a surprising way.

Whoever you are, child, you are brave. I am Miles Hendon, and I will help you!

And at that moment, a messenger arrived from the palace. Miles and the prince slipped away.

The king is dead!

Once inside, the messenger gave everyone the news.

Long live the king!

All the lords and ladies fell to their knees before the child they thought was their prince.

Meanwhile, Miles Hendon led Edward to his room in an inn on London Bridge. But John Canty had already reached the bridge and was waiting for his son.

Come here! I'll pound your bones into powder.

Not so fast!

Touch him and I'll split you like a goose! Now get out of here and be quick about it!

You just wait. You haven't seen the last of me!

When they reached Hendon's room...

The little beggar has taken my bed as if he owned it. He called himself the Prince of Wales, and it even sounds as though he believes it.

But I've taken a liking to the boy. I'll be his friend for as long as he needs me.

In the morning Miles had breakfast brought to the room.

But when he tried to sit down...

Stop! Would you sit while the king is in the room with you?

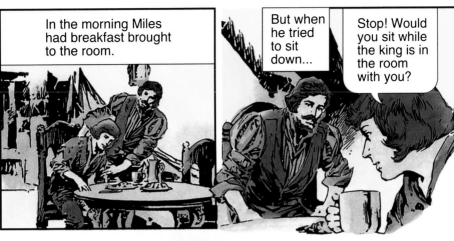

I must do as he says until his mind is better.

Tell me your story. You seem to be a truly noble man.

So Miles told Edward his story. A soldier, he had been captured and kept in prison for seven years in another country. At last he escaped and returned to England.

You are very brave. I am also sure that you have saved me from harm and even death! I owe you a great deal. Just tell me what you want.

He was just then on his way to his family home, Hendon Hall. He hoped his loved ones would be happy to see him alive after all this time.

My wish is only that I, and my family after me, may be allowed to sit when the king is present.

So Miles was finally able to sit down without offending his young friend. He even went so far as to finish up what was left of the meal!

Your wish is granted, Sir Miles Hendon. You are a knight of the crown.

Later Miles went out to buy some clothes for the boy.

But when he returned...

Where is the boy?

A young man came and said you wanted the boy to join you on the other side of London Bridge.

The boy is not to be found. He's gone! But he went looking for me. And I will search until I see him again.

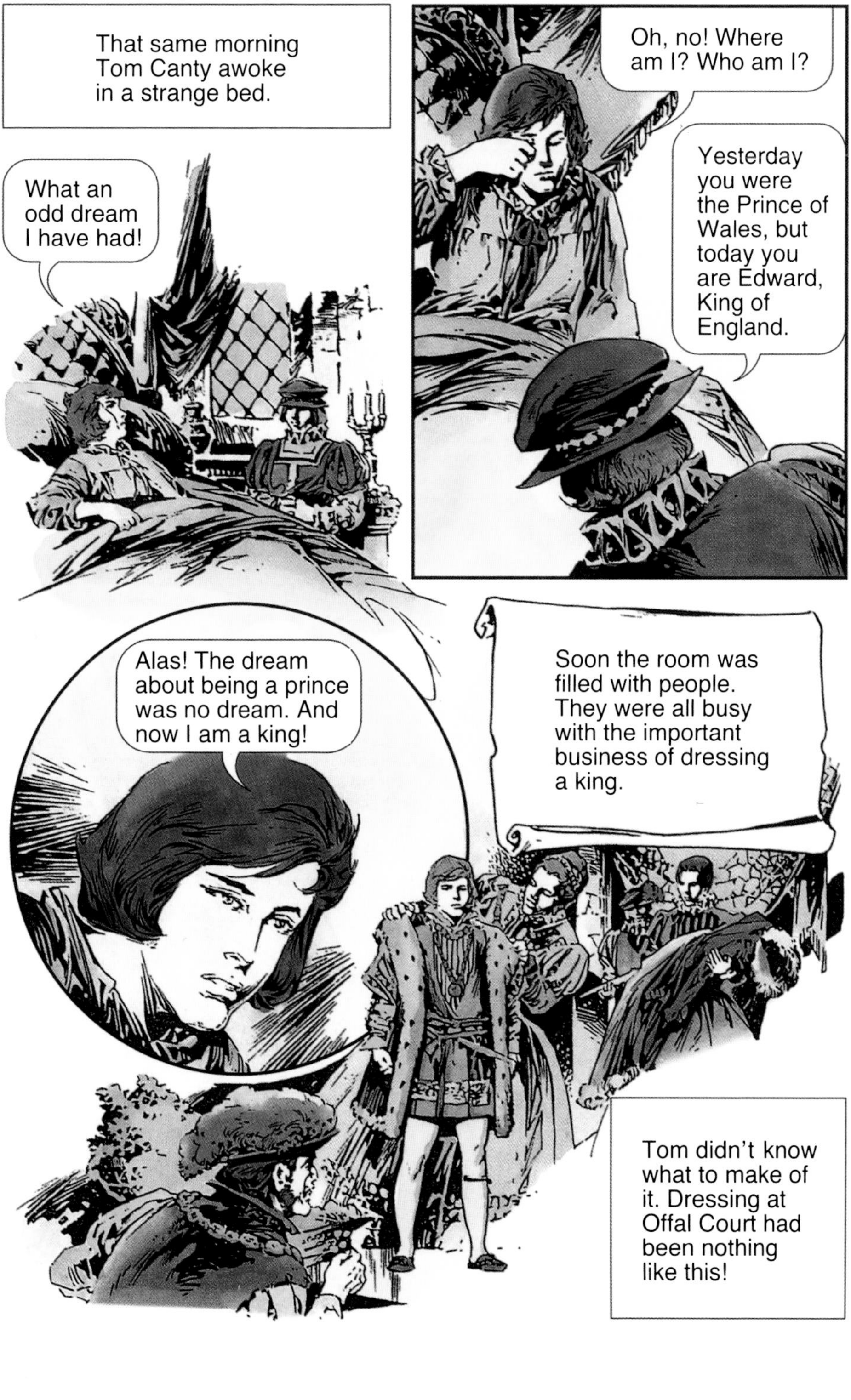
That same morning Tom Canty awoke in a strange bed.
What an odd dream I have had!
Oh, no! Where am I? Who am I?
Yesterday you were the Prince of Wales, but today you are Edward, King of England.
Alas! The dream about being a prince was no dream. And now I am a king!
Soon the room was filled with people. They were all busy with the important business of dressing a king.
Tom didn't know what to make of it. Dressing at Offal Court had been nothing like this!

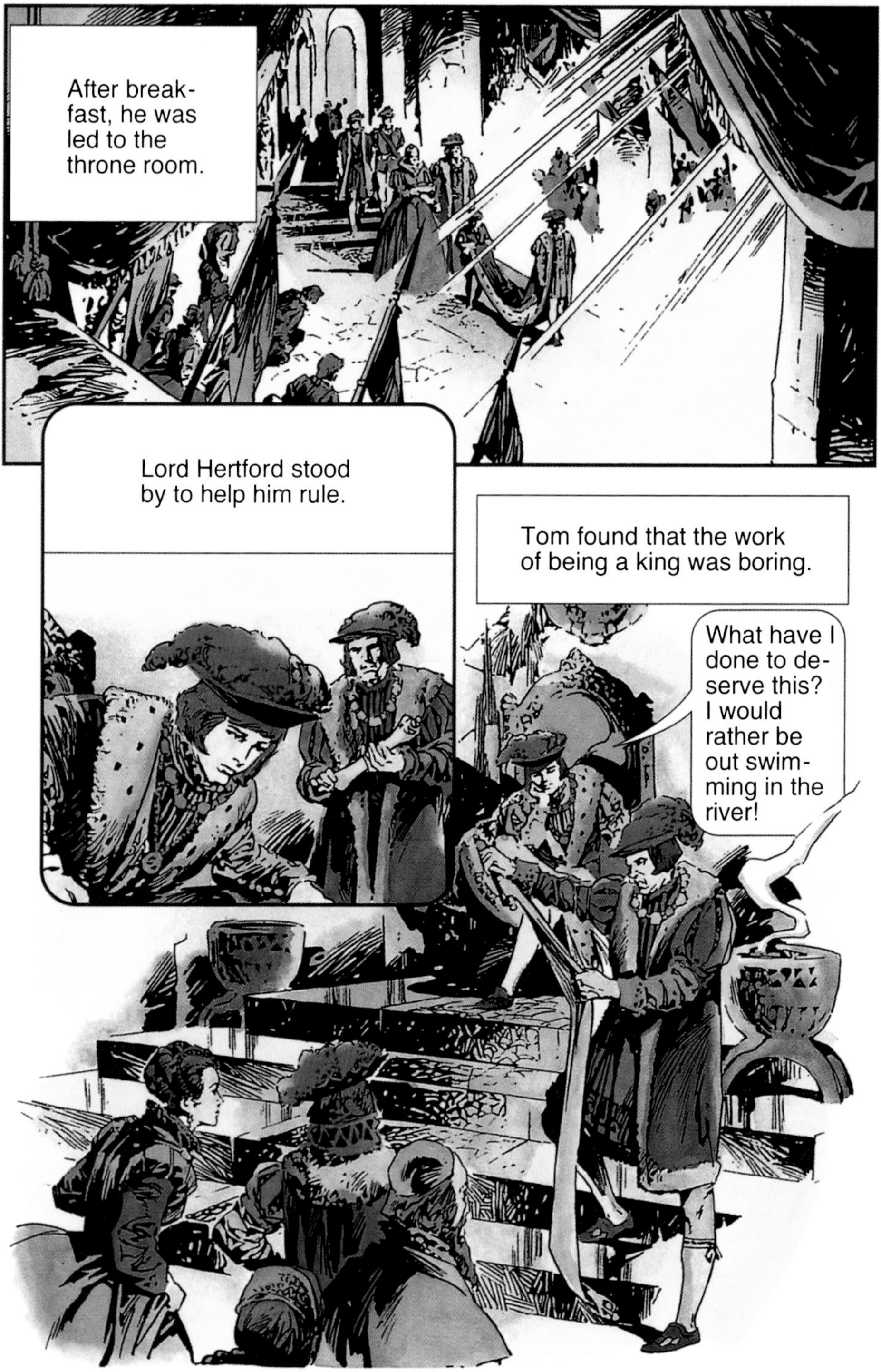
After break-
fast, he was
led to the
throne room.
Lord Hertford stood
by to help him rule.
Tom found that the work
of being a king was boring.
What have I
done to de-
serve this?
I would
rather be
out swim-
ming in the
river!

That afternoon Tom was sitting quietly in his room when a boy entered.

Who are you?

You must remember me, my lord. I am Humphrey Marlow, your whipping boy.

But why would I need a whipping boy?

No one may punish the Prince of Wales! My job is to take the whipping that should be yours when you do poorly at your lessons!

Alas, Sire, since you are no longer a prince, you will surely stop your studies. Now I will be out of work. My sisters and I will starve.

Starve? How?

Without a job as your whipping boy I will not be able to buy food for the family. How will we eat?

Tom could see that here was a boy who could help him.

Then, for more than an hour, Tom asked Humphrey everything he should know about the court.

Rise, Humphrey Marlow, grand whipping boy to the royal house of England. I will study again, and do so poorly that they will have to pay you three times what you earn now!

So the first days that Tom was king came and went. He still felt strange, but with each day he learned more and his job became easier.

One day Tom stood at the windows looking out. On the street below he saw a crowd.

I wish I knew what that is all about.

You are the king! Your wish is an order!

Soon word returned that the crowd was following some people who were to be put to death.

Bring them here!

Tom knew that visitors were waiting to see him. But he was more interested in learning about the people who were to die.

Sometimes being a king is boring; other times it is exciting!

Truly, this is how I felt when I heard Father Andrew's stories.

Have mercy. Let me be hanged!

What? Weren't you on your way to be hanged?

Oh, no, my lord! It is ordered that I be boiled alive!

Your wish is granted. No one must ever be boiled alive again!

History will remember this noble act and honor you for it.

But wait! Why is this man being put to death?

A witch said that a man who was already sick would die by being poisoned. When the sick man died, the witch said that this man had killed him.

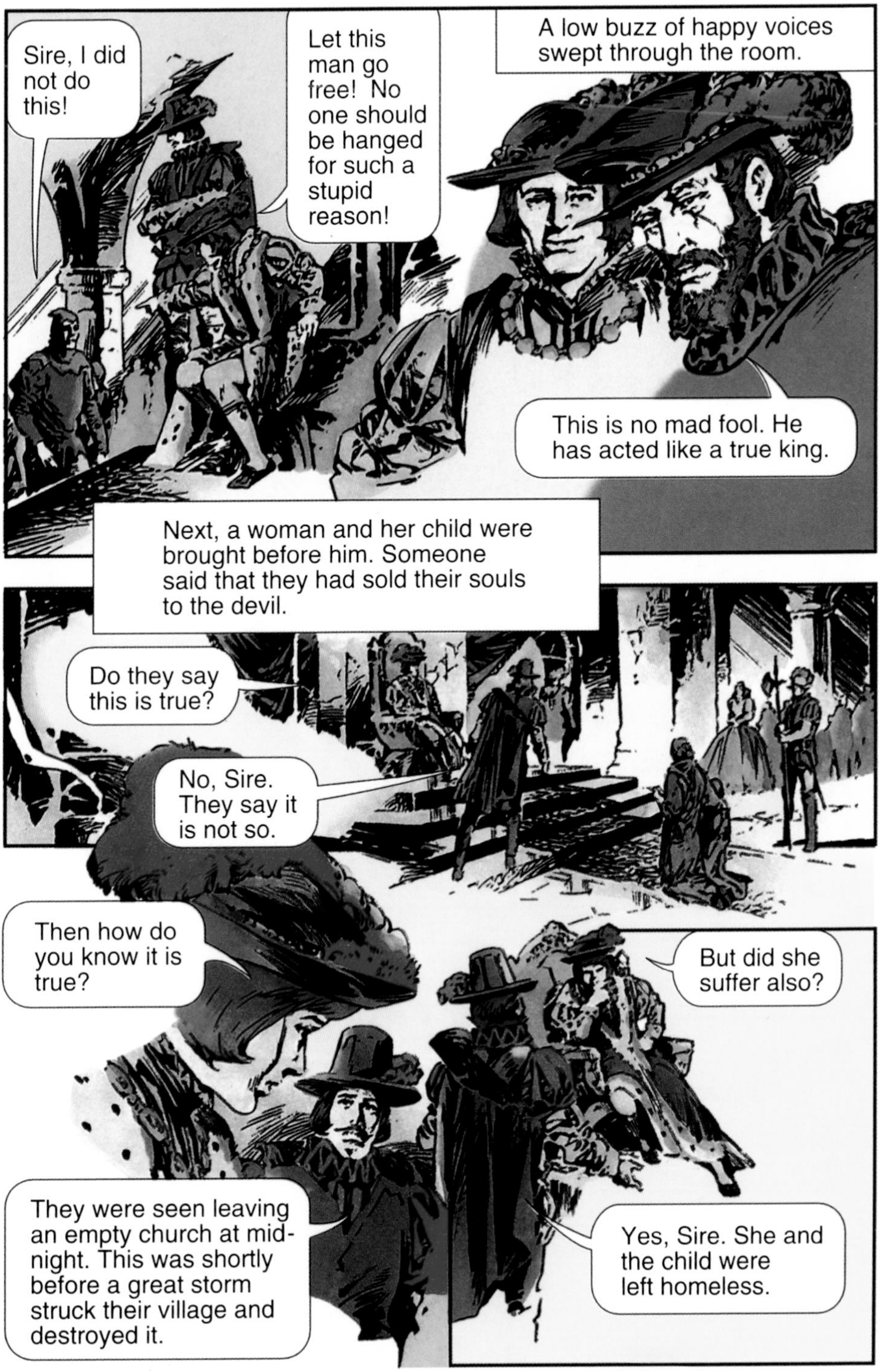
Sire, I did not do this!
Let this man go free! No one should be hanged for such a stupid reason!
A low buzz of happy voices swept through the room.
This is no mad fool. He has acted like a true king.
Next, a woman and her child were brought before him. Someone said that they had sold their souls to the devil.
Do they say this is true?
No, Sire. They say it is not so.
Then how do you know it is true?
They were seen leaving an empty church at mid-night. This was shortly before a great storm struck their village and destroyed it.
But did she suffer also?
Yes, Sire. She and the child were left homeless.

This power has cost you a great deal. Use it now to show me a storm, and you and your child shall go free.

Oh, Sire, I have no such power!

I think she has spoken the truth! If my own mother were in her place and had this power, she would use it to save the life of her child.

This man is not mad. He is a king, and a wise one.

But let us return to Miles Hendon, Edward's friend.

By asking questions Miles was able to trace the lost boy past London Bridge.

Miles Hendon had told Edward that they were going to Hendon Hall, his old home. He believed Edward would try to find him there. So Miles left London at once, searching the woods and asking about the boy as he headed for Kent.

Having been tricked into thinking that his friend Miles was hurt, Edward had followed the messenger.

Finally they reached a burned-out farmhouse. Just past it was a barn that was falling into ruin.

But when they entered...

Where is Miles?

Don't anger your father again or you'll get a beating!

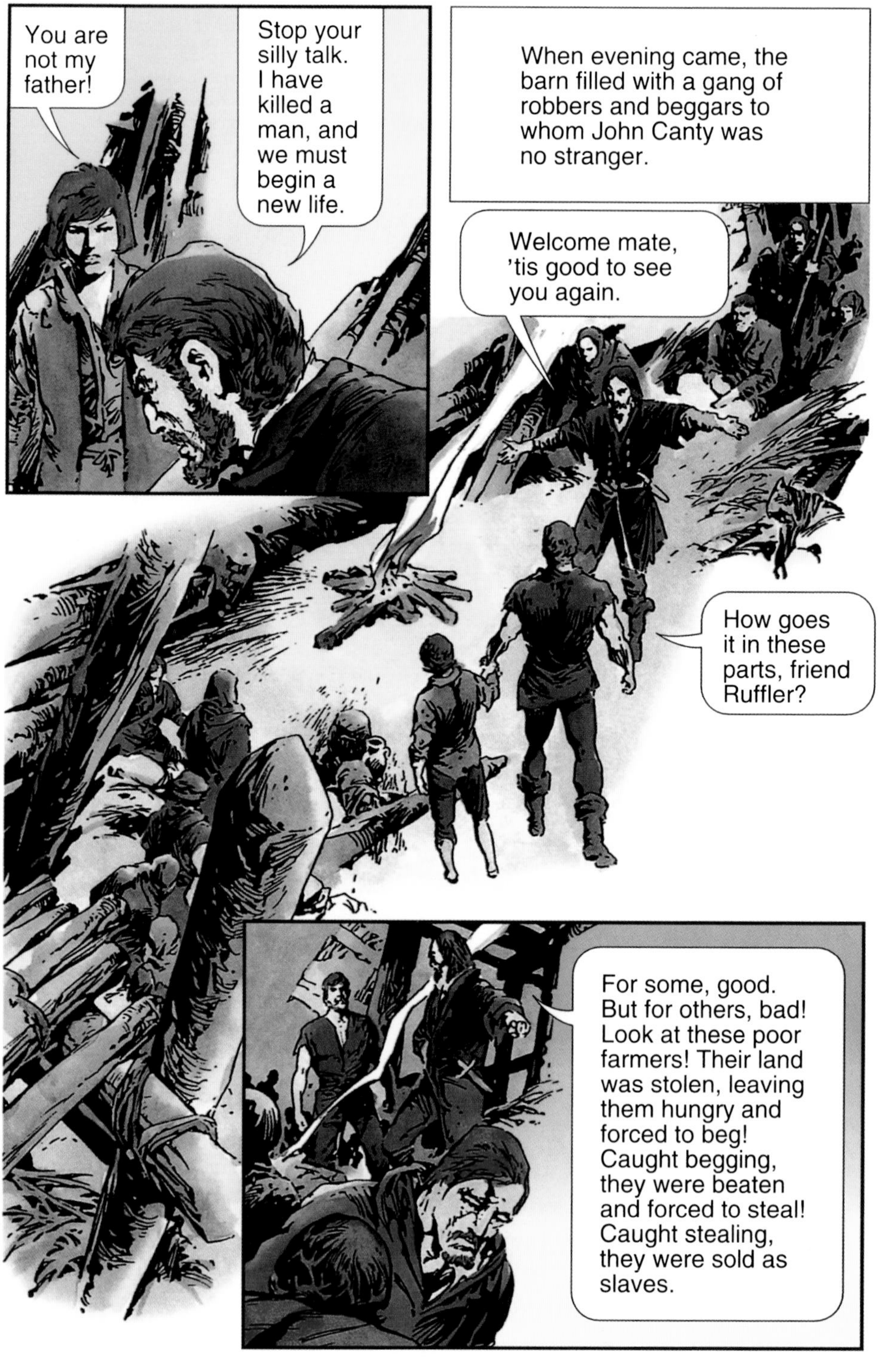

You are not my father!
Stop your silly talk. I have killed a man, and we must begin a new life.
When evening came, the barn filled with a gang of robbers and beggars to whom John Canty was no stranger.
Welcome mate, 'tis good to see you again.
How goes it in these parts, friend Ruffler?
For some, good. But for others, bad! Look at these poor farmers! Their land was stolen, leaving them hungry and forced to beg! Caught begging, they were beaten and forced to steal! Caught stealing, they were sold as slaves.

Drink, boys, to the great English Law! It has stolen my farm, killed my family, and now will hang me as a slave if I'm caught.

Edward was now learning lessons about the poor people of England that he would never have learned in his castle!

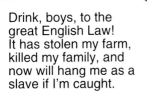

From this day, that law is no more.

Who are you?

I am Edward, King of England.

Friends, he is my son and a fool who is mad. Pay him no mind.

My, my. Have you no respect? We are bad men in some small ways, but none among us is a traitor to his king.

"As your king, I thank you, my good people."

"Drop it boy. It's not wise or well to keep this up."

"But one of the robbers had an idea for some fun."

"Let us make him our king! We will honor him!"

"All hail!"

"Long live the king of the slaves!"

Tears fell from Edward's eyes. He wanted to help these poor people, but no one had believed his story.

The next morning the robber gang headed south for the winter.

When they came to a town, they broke into smaller groups to go about their begging and stealing. Edward was ordered to go with an older boy named Hugo.

Good sir, a penny, please, to buy a little food.

You shall have three, poor child.

Come boy, help me carry your sick brother to that near-by house.

He is not my brother. He has taken your money and picked your pocket as well.

And if you would like to see him healed quickly, just hit him across the shoulders with your cane!

In a moment Hugo had jumped up and was off like the wind. Edward ran away from him down another street.

All day the young king traveled, hungry and tired.

Finally he could go no farther. He stopped at a barn and lay down to sleep next to a cow.

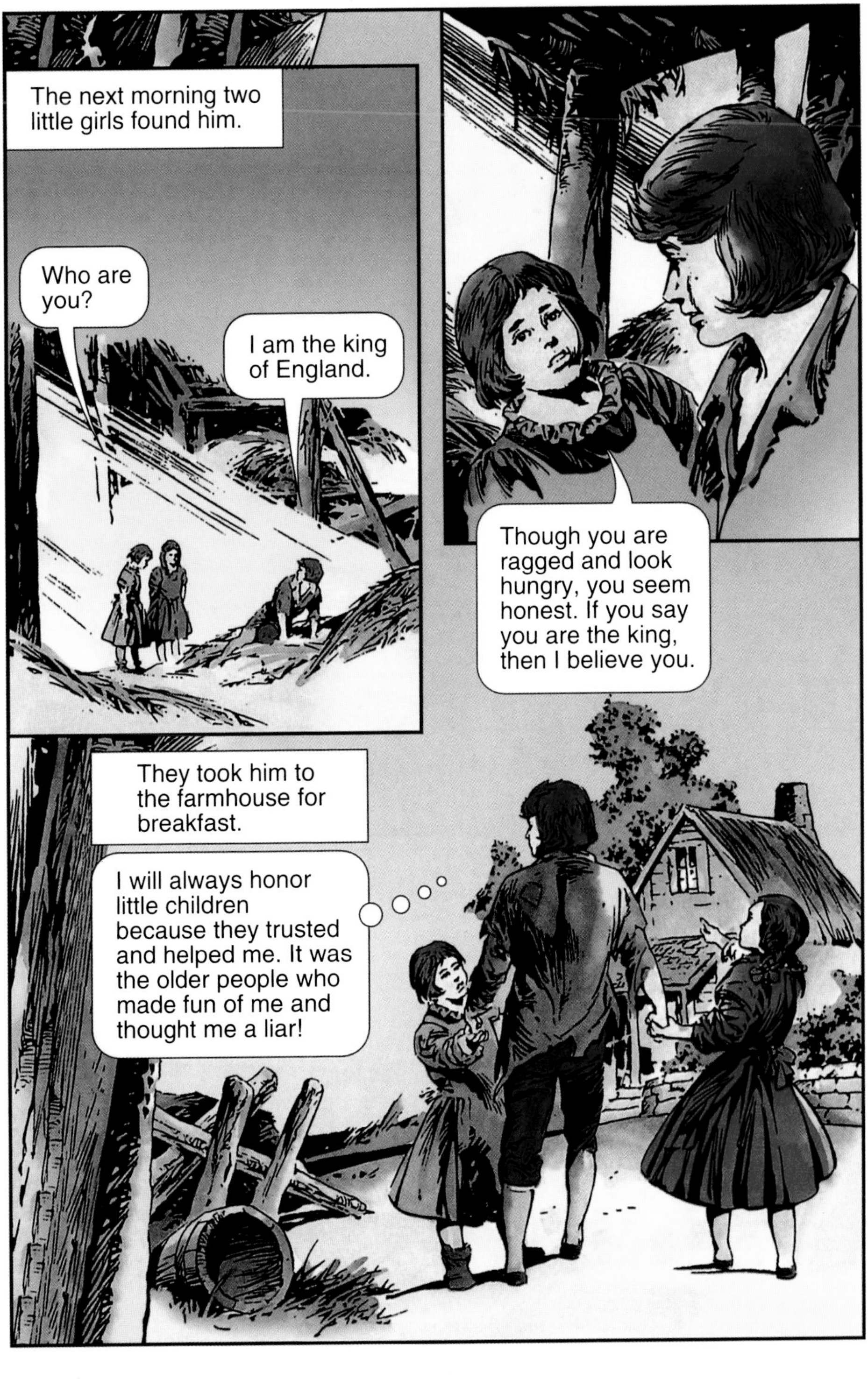
The next morning two little girls found him.
Who are you?
I am the king of England.
Though you are ragged and look hungry, you seem honest. If you say you are the king, then I believe you.
They took him to the farmhouse for breakfast.
I will always honor little children because they trusted and helped me. It was the older people who made fun of me and thought me a liar!

The children's mother gave him a good meal. She was poor herself, and knew what it was like to be hungry.

Afterward, Edward washed the dishes for her.

Edward was learning more and more about his people. This kind woman, without knowing it, taught him a great deal about true goodness.

Then, just by chance, Edward looked out the window and saw John Canty and Hugo coming toward the farmhouse.

Without a word he stepped quietly out the back door and hurried off down the lane.

He ran into the forest. The farther he went, the darker the woods became.

He traveled on and on. As night was falling, however, he saw a light.

It came from a small hut. Inside, an old man was praying.

Who are you?

I am the king.

And I am an archangel.

Oh, no! This man is mad! I would have been better off with the robbers!

But the old man treated him gently and put him to bed. Edward slept so well that he did not wake even when the hermit crept in and tied him up.

The next morning he woke to a terrible surprise. The hermit was standing over him with a knife in his hand!

Son of King Henry, do you know that it was your father who made me homeless? If he had not ordered that our monastery be closed, I might have been Pope!

But then...just in time, Edward heard a voice.

Hello. Have you seen a boy in these woods?

It was Miles Hendon.

What boy?

Tell me no lies. The people who stole him from me said they had tracked him here!

Oh, you must mean the boy who spent the night here. I sent him to do something for me.

Come, friend. You will show me where.

Inside, Edward heard their voices move away. Then everything was still.

A moment later Edward heard the door open. He closed his eyes and could almost feel the knife at his throat.

But it was John Canty and Hugo.

Quickly they untied him. Before the boy could catch his breath, they were hurrying away with him through the forest.

So once again the "king of the slaves" had joined Ruffler's band of robbers.

Hugo, however, was still angry with Edward for what he had done while they were begging. He decided to trick Edward into getting caught by the police.

The next day Hugo robbed a package from a woman whose back was turned. Before she turned around again, Hugo tossed it to Edward and ran away.

Quickly a crowd closed around the king. Just then...

Let go of that boy, woman.

Well, it's about time you found me, Sir Miles.

A policeman arrived. In moments they all stood in court before a judge.

What is that package worth?

Forty-four cents, your honor.

Do you know that a person can be hanged for stealing anything worth more than thirteen and a half cents?

What have I done? If you wish, say that the package is worth only eight cents. But do not hang the child!

The judge spoke kindly to Edward. Finally he and Miles were free.

With luck and a little money, Miles was able to find a mule and a donkey for their journey. So they shared the stories of their adventures as they rode toward Hendon Hall.

Miles spoke of his wise old father and his older brother Arthur. He spoke also of his cousin Edith whom he loved. He even had kind words for his younger brother, Hugh, whom he had never really liked. Finally...

There is the village! And on the hill beyond is Hendon Hall. Let us hurry!

Having been so long away from home, Miles was overjoyed to be returning at last.

Reaching the court- yard, Miles helped Edward off his donkey.

Welcome to Hendon Hall, my king! My father and brother Arthur will be mad for joy to see me home safely! I expect even Hugh will be pleased!

Inside, Miles found his younger brother.

Here I am, Hugh. I am home!

Who are you? How do you know my name?

I am your brother, Miles Hendon.

You do look a little like my brother. But a letter I once received tells me that you are not.

What letter?

One that came from over the sea six or seven years ago. It said my brother died in battle.

That is a lie! Call my father and my brother Arthur.

I cannot call back the dead.

This is sorry news. But do not tell me Lady Edith is also...

No, she is alive. I will go and get her.

You have company, good friend. I, too, am having trouble trying to prove who I am.

Oh, Edith, my darling!

Do you know this stranger?

The lady trembled for several moments, then spoke in a voice like death.

The servants shook their heads. Edith ran from the room.

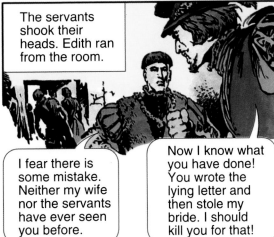

I do not know him.

And you, servants, do you know who this man is?

I fear there is some mistake. Neither my wife nor the servants have ever seen you before.

Now I know what you have done! You wrote the lying letter and then stole my bride. I should kill you for that!

No! Stop him, you servants!

Get away from me! I will not shame myself by fighting with the likes of you!

I have a plan. I will write a letter in Latin, Greek, and English. Tomorrow you will take it to my uncle, Lord Hertford. He will know I wrote it and will send for me at once. Then I will give back all that was yours.

Poor mad boy! His mind is still busy with that crazy dream!

Soon Edward handed Miles the finished letter. But just at that moment, armed guards rushed into the room and ran at them. In the struggle that followed, Miles forgot all about Edward's letter.

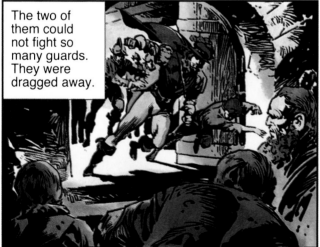

The two of them could not fight so many guards. They were dragged away.

Poor Miles had come home expecting a joyous welcome. Instead, he found himself in jail.

Again and again he thought of Edith. He wondered why she had pretended not to know him. Had she been forced to act that way?

Every day the jailer brought people in to insult Miles. In doing this, Hugh was trying to build a case against his brother.

A week passed. Then...

It's Blake Andrews, a good and honest family servant.

Thank goodness you are alive. Say the word, and I'll speak out, even though I be hanged for it!

It would do no good to say that you know me. But thank you for offering to do so.

Every day Andrews returned and brought his master food.

He told Miles how Hugh had tricked his dying father into making Edith marry him. And he told how his brother had become cruel and heartless toward all.

When his trial came, Miles was sentenced to
sit for two hours in the stocks. This made
Edward very angry.

No! Let him alone! Whip me instead!

A good idea! Let the little beggar go, but make it a full dozen for this fellow.

Edward wept while Miles took the beating in silence. After that, even the mob in the jailyard thought well of him.

Dear friend, I thank you again. For this I will make you an earl of the kingdom!

Poor crazy child! Yet I love him for what he gives from his heart.

Meanwhile, Hugh rode off, and a deep quiet fell over the crowd.

Two hours later Miles was freed and ordered never to return. The crowd parted to let him pass.

Where are we going, Sire?

To London!

A few days later they entered London. It was the evening before the Prince of Wales was to be crowned king of England. In the huge crowd Edward and Miles became separated.

By midnight Tom Canty was sleeping soundly. In his dreams he was already the king.

At the same hour, however, Edward, the true king, was hungry and tired. Sadly he watched the workmen at Westminster Abbey finish preparing for the next day's crowning.

At dawn, crowds lined the streets. A grand parade moved through the city passing under one great arch after another.

All of this is to welcome me!

Suddenly Tom heard a voice from his past.

Oh my child, my darling!

Good woman, I do not know you!

The grand parade moved on. But for Tom Canty, the thought of his mother, left behind, spoiled the joy of his day.

Shake off this sadness, my prince; the eyes of the world are upon you.

The parade reached Westminster Abbey and the crowning began. Tom Canty was about to become king.

A deep hush fell upon the crowd. Every eye looked toward Tom, when suddenly...

Do not crown that head! I am the king!

No! Do not touch him; he is the king!

Oh, my lord the king, let poor Tom Canty be the first to show you honor.

If you are the king, you will have to prove it!

Where is the Great Seal? Only the true Prince of Wales could know.

Very well. St. John, go to my private room in the palace. In the left corner farthest from the door is a brass nail. Press it and a secret door will open. The seal is inside. Bring it here!

All were amazed to see the young beggar pick out a nobleman, call him by name, and speak as if he knew him well. But when the man returned...

The seal is not there.

56

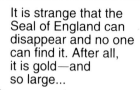
It is strange that the Seal of England can disappear and no one can find it. After all, it is gold—and so large...

What! Was it round and thick?

Remember, Sire, when you saw my hurt hand and jumped up to punish the guard? You saw the Seal on the table and looked for a place to hide it...

Yes.

I know where it is, but I did not put it there.

Yes! I remember now!

Go, my good St. John. In the armpiece of the suit of armor you will find the Great Seal.

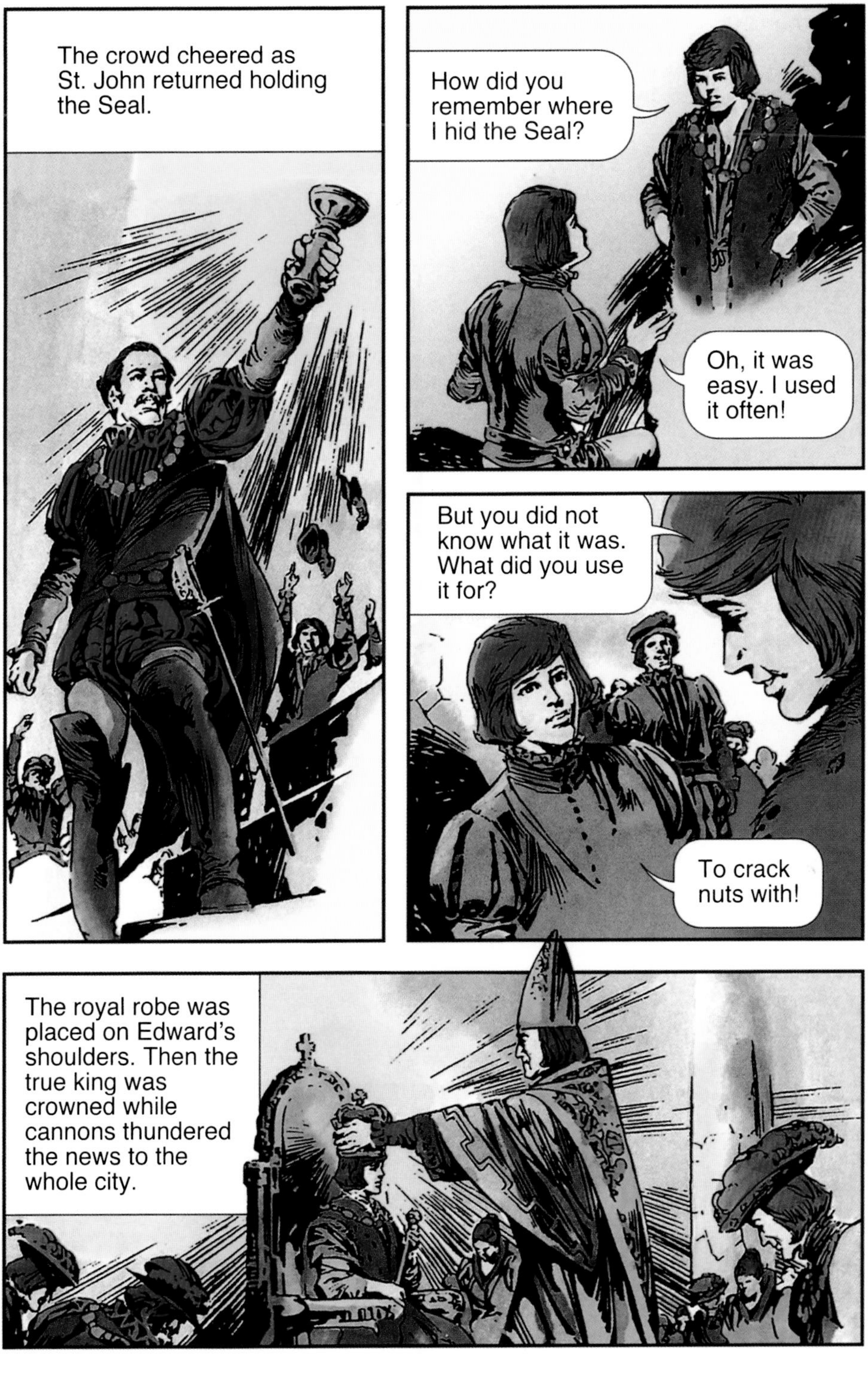
The crowd cheered as St. John returned holding the Seal.
How did you remember where I hid the Seal?
Oh, it was easy. I used it often!
But you did not know what it was. What did you use it for?
To crack nuts with!
The royal robe was placed on Edward's shoulders. Then the true king was crowned while cannons thundered the news to the whole city.

At that moment, Miles Hendon was far away on the bank of the river. He was tired from an all-night search for his lost friend.

He heard the far-off boom of the cannons and thought to himself, "The new king is crowned." Then he fell asleep.

When he awoke he set out for the palace to find an old friend of his father's who might help him.

But he was soon arrested and searched. The guards found only a scrap of paper in his pocket.

Hold this man while I take his letter to the king.

Miles smiled when he remembered that this was the letter his crazy young friend had given him.

Soon the guard returned. This time he spoke gently to Miles.

Please follow me, sir.

Can this be true? Is that really my young friend on the throne of England?

Suddenly he had a wild idea. He found a chair and sat down in the middle of the hall.

Touch him not! It is his right. This is my good servant Sir Miles Hendon. I now name him Earl of Kent and give him gold and lands to match his title.

Just then Sir Hugh and Lady Edith reached the great hall.

Take from this robber his stolen lands and put him under lock and key.

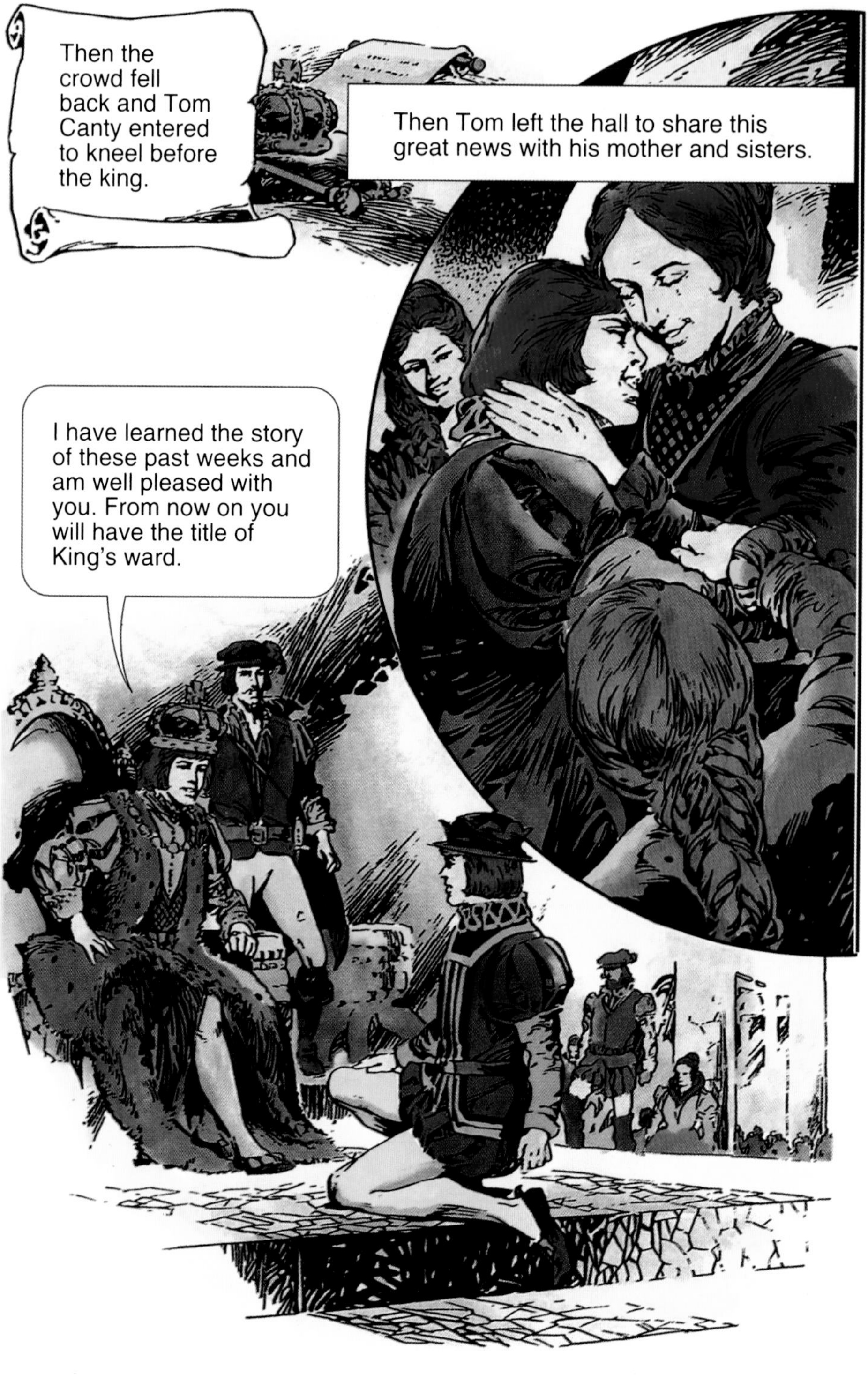
Then the crowd fell back and Tom Canty entered to kneel before the king.
Then Tom left the hall to share this great news with his mother and sisters.
I have learned the story of these past weeks and am well pleased with you. From now on you will have the title of King's ward.

Meanwhile, Edith told Miles how Hugh had forced her to lie when he had appeared at Hendon Hall. In the end, however, Hugh ran off to Europe leaving Edith behind. Shortly afterward he died.

By and by Miles, the Earl of Kent, married Edith. All the people of Hendon Village were happy for them.

As king, Edward showed himself a merciful ruler. More than once he grew angry with some fancy lord who spoke against the king's kind ways.

What do you know of suffering? I and my people know, but you do not!

The END